D0189280

Aberdeenshire Library and Information Service
www.aberdeenshire.gov.uk/libraries
Renewals Hotline 01224 661511

2 7 FEB 2~   ~T 2009   ~3 NOV 2010

  ~1 APR 2~   ~5 JAN 2011

1 8 APR 2009   ~ DEC 2009   2 6 FEB 2011
                  2 7 FEB 2010

                  2 7 MAR 2010   ~2 APR 2011
  ~9 MAY 2009   2 3 APR 2010
                                                1 4 MAY 2011

  ~5 JUN 2009   ~3 JUN 2011

                  2 6 MAY 2010   ~4 JUL 2011
                  2 8 JUN 2010   ~1 AUG 2011

1 8 JUL 2009
   1 0 AUG 2009   1 6 AUG 2010   1 9 AUG 2011
   2 6 SEP 2009   2 3 AUG 2010   1 3 SEP 2011

                  2 2 SEP 2010   1 9 NOV 2011
                                      1 6 DEC 2011
                                      1 8 JAN 2012

         ALBOROUGH, Jez   1 4 APR 2012
                                      2 6 MAY 2012
         It's the bear!   ~3 JUL 2012

                                      3 1 AUG 2012

A L I S

2640869

For David, Amelia,
Jane, Jason and Lucy
with thanks

ABERDEENSHIRE LIBRARY AND	
INFORMATION SERVICES	
2640869	
HJ	720154
JP	£5.99
JU	SURB

First published 1994 by Walker Books Ltd
87 Vauxhall Walk, London SE11 5HJ

This edition published 2004

4 6 8 10 9 7 5

© 1994 Jez Alborough

The right of Jez Alborough to be identified as
author/illustrator of this work has been asserted by him in
accordance with the Copyright, Designs and Patents Act 1988

This book has been typeset in Garamond

Printed in China

All rights reserved. No part of this book may be reproduced,
transmitted or stored in an information retrieval system in
any form or by any means, graphic, electronic or mechanical,
including photocopying, taping and recording, without
prior written permission from the publisher.

British Library Cataloguing in Publication Data:
a catalogue record for this book
is available from the British Library

ISBN-13: 978-1-84428-475-7

www.walkerbooks.co.uk

It's the Bear!

JEZ ALBOROUGH

WALKER BOOKS
AND SUBSIDIARIES
LONDON • BOSTON • SYDNEY • AUCKLAND

Eddy doesn't want to come
and picnic in the woods with Mum.

"I'm scared," he said, "about the bear, the great big bear that lives in there."

"A bear?" said Mum. "That's silly, dear!
We don't get great big bears round here."

"There's just you and me and your teddy, Freddy.
Now let's all get the picnic ready."

"We've got lettuce,
tomatoes,
creamy cheese spread,
with hard-boiled eggs
and crusty brown bread.
There's orange juice,
biscuits,
some crisps and –

OH MY!

I've forgotten to pack
the blueberry pie..."

"I'll pop back and get it,"
she said. "Won't be long."
"BUT MUM!"
gasped Eddy …

too late –
SHE HAD GONE!

He sat on the hamper
and tried not to cry,
then…

"*I CAN SMELL FOOD!*"
yelled a voice
from nearby.

"IT'S THE BEAR!"
cried Eddy.
"WHERE CAN I HIDE?"

Then he opened
the hamper and
clambered inside.

Out of the trees
stepped a big hungry bear,
licking his lips
and sniffing the air.
"A teddy bear's picnic,"
he bellowed. "Hooray!"
"Help," whispered Eddy.
"He's coming this way."

He cuddled
his teddy,
he huddled
and hid ...

then a great big
bear bottom

sat down on the lid.

The bear munched
and he crunched,
he chomped
and he chewed,
and greedily gobbled up
all of the food.

"Now what's for dessert?"
said the bear.
"Let me see…"

"Oh, please,"
whimpered Eddy,
    "don't let it be me."

"Don't let him see me!
DON'T LET HIM COME..."

"Eddy, I'm coming," called Mum. "Are you hurt?"
"It's the bear," cried Eddy. "He thinks I'm dessert!"

"A bear?" said Mum. "I told you, my dear.
Your Freddy's the only bear round here."

"*NO HE'S NOT!*"
screamed Eddy.
"*BEHIND YOU,
IT'S THERE!*"
"Don't be silly,"
said Mum.
"There can't
be …
there just
can't be …
there isn't …"

"I *TOLD* you!" cried Eddy.
"RUN!" shouted Mum.
"Blueberry pie," said the bear.
"I *LOVE* it…"